For Richard – *J.K.*
For Jessica and Rosie – *C.W.*
For Jenny, Ella and Sam – *P.D.*

First published in Great Britain in 2006 and in the USA in 2007
by Frances Lincoln Children's Books, 4 Torriano Mews,
Torriano Avenue, London NW5 2RZ

www.franceslincoln.com

Distributed in the USA by Publishers Group West

British Library Cataloguing in Publication Data available on request

ISBN 10: 1-84507-449-1
ISBN 13: 978-1-84507-449-4

Printed in Singapore

1 3 5 7 9 8 6 4 2

Time to Say
I Love You

Jane Kemp & Clare Walters
Illustrated by **Penny Dale**

F
FRANCES LINCOLN
CHILDREN'S BOOKS

When's the best time to say I love you?

Shall I say it when you wake me with a kiss?

Shall I say it when you're
riding tall upon my shoulders?

Shall I say it when we're
chasing waves across the sand?

Shall I say it when we're
climbing high up on the hill?

Shall I say it when we're
painting pictures in the clouds?

Shall I say it when we're
dashing homewards through the rain?

Shall I say it when we're curled up close
beside the fire?

Shall I say it when we're gazing at the stars?

When is the best time to say I love you?

Right now. I LOVE YOU!